Puppy in Peril

Lucy Daniels

With special thanks to Janet Bingham
For Denny

ORCHARD BOOKS

First published in Great Britain in 2018 by The Watts Publishing Group

1 3 5 7 9 10 8 6 4 2

Text copyright © Working Partners Ltd, 2018
Illustrations copyright © Working Partners Ltd, 2018

A CIP catalogue record for this book
is available from the British Library.

ISBN 978 1 40835 404 9

Printed and bound in Great Britain by CPI Group (UK) Ltd, Croydon, CR0 4YY

The paper and board used in this book are made from wood from responsible sources.

Orchard Books
An imprint of
Hachette Children's Group
Part of The Watts Publishing Group Limited
Carmelite House
50 Victoria Embankment
London EC4Y 0DZ

An Hachette UK Company
www.hachette.co.uk
www.hachettechildrens.co.uk

CONTENTS

Puppy in Peril

CHAPTER ONE

"Sit, Mac!" said Sam Baxter. The Westie puppy sat back, and even though his waggy bottom didn't *quite* reach the floor, Amelia Haywood cheered.

"You're doing a great job training him, Sam," she told her best friend. She couldn't believe the difference in Mac after just a few weeks. When she had first met Sam, his puppy had seemed really naughty.

"I can't believe that's the same little dog that once tried to eat my shoes," said Julia Kaminski, the receptionist at Animal Ark vet's surgery. They were in the waiting room of the surgery, next to Julia's desk. She wheeled over and took Mac's lead from Sam, then looped it over a hook on the wall. "Mac will be fine here with me – won't you, sweetie?"

Amelia and Sam each patted Mac's shaggy white coat and stroked his pricked-up ears. Then they went through to the section of Animal Ark that was nicknamed the hotel, where the animals staying overnight were kept. They passed a pen with a pair of rabbits inside, and another pen that held a spotty Dalmatian dog with a bandaged tail.

Amelia could feel her heart soaring. She and her mum had moved to Welford a few weeks ago, after her parents split up, and Animal Ark was already her favourite place in the village.

Mr and Mrs Hope, the vets who

owned Animal Ark, were standing by one of the pens. Inside it were Caramel, a beautiful tortoiseshell cat, and her four kittens. Amelia and Sam had rescued them, and today was a special day.

"Hello, you two," said Mr Hope, his kind eyes crinkling as he grinned.

"You're just in time to see them off to their new homes," said Mrs Hope. Her red hair hung over one shoulder as she arranged three cat baskets and three bags full of sachets of kitten food on a table. There were leaflets sticking out about cat care as well.

Amelia looked up at the clock on the wall. It was almost nine o'clock, and time for the new owners to come and pick up their kittens. She was happy for them, of course, but a bit sad too. She'd miss the kittens when they were gone!

Amelia went over to Caramel's pen. She took out the ginger kitten. When she and Sam had first found them, the

11

kittens had been tiny enough to pick up with one hand, but they'd already more than doubled in size. The ginger kitten purred and kneaded the air, showing the pink pads on his paws.

Amelia heard more voices coming from reception, and Julia saying, "Go right on through. They're waiting."

Amelia and Sam's friend Josh came in to the room.

"Hi!" he said, smiling at them. Amelia kissed the kitten's head. "Your new pet!" she said.

"Hi, Flash," said Josh, taking the kitten from Amelia. Josh loved taking photos, and he'd named his kitten after the flash of a camera. Flash's ginger fur was almost exactly the same shade as Josh's own hair.

An elderly lady wearing a long purple scarf came in next. "Hello, Mrs Cranbourne," said Amelia and Sam together. She was followed closely by Mr Stevens, the farmer, in his mud-spattered jacket. They greeted him too.

When they'd first met Mrs Cranbourne they thought she was really grumpy, but now they knew how much she loved animals. Sam carefully picked up one of

13

the tortoiseshell kittens, making sure he'd
got the right one, and passed it to her.

"Hello, Miss Fizz," said Mrs
Cranbourne, snuggling the kitten
against her cheek. Miss Fizz
mewed and touched Mrs
Cranbourne's nose with
her own tiny nose.

"Isn't this exciting?" said
Mr Stevens.

"It's time to go
to your new home,
Snowdrop." Amelia
picked up another tortoiseshell kitten,
who had a white tip on her tail, and
put her in the third basket. Sam scooped

up the kittens' mother. At first Caramel
didn't want to go into the basket, and
wriggled in Sam's arms. But when
Amelia put a cat treat inside, Caramel
quickly jumped in with Snowdrop.

Mr Hope held open the door, and
Josh, Mrs Cranbourne and Mr Stevens
went out with their new pets and bags
of kitten food.

"Thank you!" called Mr Stevens.

"I'll let you know how Miss Fizz
settles in," said Mrs Cranbourne with a
wide smile.

"Come and visit Flash soon!" added
Josh.

Amelia felt warmth spread through

her like sunshine. *It's brilliant that they've all got loving new homes*, she thought.

But from the pen came a sad mew. One tortoiseshell kitten remained, the one Amelia secretly called Star because of the star-shaped white patch above her eyes.

"Poor kitty," said Sam, wiggling a piece of string into the pen for her to play with.

"Hasn't anyone said they want to adopt her?" asked Amelia.

"Not yet," said Mrs Hope.

"We need the pen for our patients," added Mr Hope. "This little one isn't poorly, so we can't keep her here for too much longer. If we don't find someone to adopt her soon, she'll have to go to a cat sanctuary."

Amelia's heart sank. She reached into the pen to tickle the kitten's soft, fluffy head. Her golden eyes moved from Amelia to Sam, and back again.

"Three out of four kittens isn't bad," said Mrs Hope.

Amelia nodded, but inside she was determined. *I* will *find you a home, Star.*

CHAPTER TWO

Julia put her head round the door. "A new patient's just come in," she told the Hopes. "Jane Andrews brought it here. I think you'd better hurry."

The two vets went quickly through to the consulting room. Amelia and Sam followed and peeked in, watching quietly.

A woman, who Amelia realised must be Jane Andrews, was wearing a checked shirt and holding a puppy. The little dog rested her head on the woman's arm, and stared at the floor with dull eyes. Her sides rose and fell rapidly as she panted.

"She isn't mine," Jane explained. "I found her at the service station by the motorway, wandering around the car park. There's no tag on her collar, so I brought her in."

"You did the right thing," said Mrs Hope, nodding.

Jane gently laid the puppy on the examining table. The little dog whined sadly. Mr Hope ran his hands over the

puppy's head, down each leg, and along
her back and sides. "No broken bones,"
he said. When he gently felt her tummy,
he frowned. "I can feel something here.
We'll need to take an X-ray to be sure,
but I think she might need an operation."

"Oh, poor thing," Jane said, stroking the puppy's ears.

"Let's find out who you belong to," said Mrs Hope. She waved a wand-shaped microchip reader over the puppy's back. Amelia waited for it to beep, but it didn't. "Oh dear," said Mrs Hope. "She isn't chipped either. That's going to make it difficult to find her owner. I don't think she's a stray – she looks well fed."

"You can still make her better, can't you?" asked Amelia.

Mr Hope grimaced. "I'm afraid it's not that simple. Animal operations can be expensive."

"How expensive?" asked Sam.

Mr Hope looked at his wife, who placed a gentle hand on the dog. "Julia will be able to say exactly, but I'd guess about two thousand pounds. We're fully booked, so we'd have to get a specialist in to help with such a young puppy."

"But …" said Amelia. She'd have given all her pocket money for a year to help the poor animal, but that wouldn't even be two-hundred pounds. Two thousand pounds was so much money! "But what will happen if you don't operate?" she asked, trying to keep her voice steady.

The sad look on the vets' faces told her everything she needed to know.

"Amelia, sometimes animals die," said Mrs Hope. "It's something we have to accept. But don't worry – we'd make her comfortable with pain medication."

Amelia's chest felt tight with worry, and tears sprang into her eyes. It didn't seem right that all it came down to was money.

Beside her, Sam's eyes were wide. "We've got to do something," he said.

Amelia nodded, wiping a tear away with a hand. "Come on!" she said. "We'll find the puppy's owner so she can have her treatment!"

CHAPTER THREE

Amelia picked up one of the posters as they came out of the printer. She and Sam were in the office in the Old Mill Bed and Breakfast, which was run by Sam's parents. Amelia grinned, pleased. The posters had a photo of the puppy and big eye-catching lettering saying

"DOG FOUND", plus details of where she'd turned up and Animal Ark's contact information. They had already printed a pile of flyers, which were stacked on the desk next to a pot plant.

"*Someone's* got to recognise her," Amelia said. Mac was by their feet, watching them, his tail thumping the carpet. "Isn't that right, Mac?"

The puppy sprang up on to the desk. The flyers scattered and Mac snapped at them.

"Mac, no!" cried Sam.

Amelia rushed to catch the scattered flyers. Sam reached for Mac, but he pranced along the desk. His wagging tail struck the pot plant, which tottered for a moment before overbalancing. Soil spilled out as it hit the carpet, but luckily the pot didn't break.

"Bad dog!" Sam grabbed his puppy. "Oh, Mac. I thought you'd stopped being naughty. That plant is my mum's favourite one!"

Sam's face crumpled, as if he might cry – and Amelia knew why. His parents had said that unless Mac's behaviour improved, Sam wouldn't be allowed to keep him.

"Don't worry," said Amelia, kneeling down and scooping soil back into the pot. She plucked off a broken flower stem and put the plant back on the desk. "There – now no one will ever know."

Sam's expression brightened. "Do you

really think so?" he asked hopefully.

Mac licked his face and Sam smiled. It was impossible to stay angry with the puppy for long.

"Definitely," said Amelia.

Mac scrambled free and trotted to the window, where he stood on his hind legs, his front paws on the sill. He barked excitedly at something outside.

Amelia and Sam went to see what had drawn Mac's attention. A group of men and women were climbing out of a big van parked in the B&B's driveway. One man opened the doors at the back of the van, and started passing equipment out to the others. Amelia

could see lots of poles and tripods, black
umbrella-like hoods, giant lamps … and
enormous cameras.

"Wow!" said Amelia. "It looks like a
film crew!"

Sam grinned. "Let's go and see why
they're here!"

They hurried outside to find out more,
Mac bounding beside them.

Outside, Sam's mum, Mrs Baxter, was
talking to the new arrivals. "It looks like
it's going to rain," she said. "Let's get you
inside and settled in."

The crew bustled about, carrying their
equipment into the B&B. Mac sniffed
at a camera, and Sam picked him up

quickly before he could get into mischief.

Mrs Baxter beckoned them over. "This is my son, Sam," she told the film crew, "and his friend, Amelia."

"And this is Mac," said Sam.

"Hi, guys!" said a tall woman with short dark hair, dressed in skinny jeans and a leather jacket. "I'm Freya Ward.

We're staying here for a couple of days while we do some filming."

"Cool!" said Sam.

"What are you filming?" asked Amelia.

"We're doing a segment on the countryside for a TV show," said Freya. "We're filming a motorbike holiday."

"Motorcycling?" boomed a voice from behind Amelia.

She turned around to see Mr Ferguson coming outside. He was a regular guest at the B&B, and Amelia often saw him polishing his motorcycle, wearing his leather bike gear. He was bald and broad, and always made Amelia think of a grizzly bear.

"I have a rather nice motorbike myself," Mr Ferguson went on. "I've shown it off at quite a few bike shows. Happy to be in a few shots if you like."

Freya smiled at him politely. "Er ... oh ... perhaps."

Amelia winked at Sam. Mr Ferguson, who was usually in a bad mood, was beaming for a change.

They all helped get the TV equipment indoors, just as big drops of rain began to spatter on the driveway.

"Urgh – we're going to get soaked delivering these," said Sam, holding a pile of flyers.

"Oh, how sad!" said Freya, picking up one of the flyers. "I hope you find the owner soon."

"We will," said Amelia determinedly. "A little puppy is counting on us!"

CHAPTER FOUR

They spent the afternoon sloshing
through Welford in the rain, posting a
flyer through every door. The sky was
dark with thick clouds, and water was
trickling along the roads. When a car
went past, they had to dart aside to avoid
the spray churned up by its wheels.

Amelia kept the flyers and posters as dry as she could beneath her pawprint-patterned umbrella. Mac was wearing a little red raincoat, but he jumped in so many puddles that mud crept up the white fur of his legs. Soon it looked like he was wearing four dirty socks.

Amelia put the last flyer through the letterbox of a large house. "Now we need to put up the posters," she said. "Somewhere they'll stay dry."

"The bus shelter?" suggested Sam from beneath his hood. "We could try the village hall and the shop, too."

"Good plan," said Amelia.

The rain grew even heavier as they walked through the village. "Uh-oh — look who's coming!" said Sam.

It was Tiffany, a girl in their class at school. She was walking up the pavement in a pair of sparkly pink wellington boots, carefully avoiding the puddles. She wore a turquoise bomber

jacket and carried a pink umbrella that matched her boots. Her shining chestnut hair was pulled into a sleek, bouncing ponytail. Amelia sighed. She didn't know Tiffany very well, but every time they'd spoken, the other girl seemed to say something mean.

"Hi, Tiffany," said Sam unenthusiastically.

"Oh, it's you two," said Tiffany with a disdainful sniff.

Mac yapped and dashed up to her, shaking a shower of water droplets from his raincoat.

"Ugh!" Tiffany jumped back, her nose wrinkling. "Get your dog away from me! I don't want to get wet. And I don't want Sparkle to get wet either!"

"Who's Sparkle?" asked Amelia, exchanging a puzzled look with Sam.

With a smirk, Tiffany turned around. She was wearing a square pink backpack. The backpack had a mesh window, and looking out of it was a white, curly-haired puppy with a blue ribbon on its head. Amelia blinked, her mouth opening in surprise.

"Whoa!" said Sam. "There's a dog in your backpack!"

Tiffany turned back round. "It's not a backpack," she said. "It's a Canine Carrier. Sparkle is a Bichon Frise so his fur is perfectly white. You hate getting dirty, don't you, Sparkle Barkle?" She glanced at Mac, who was jumping up and down, trying to see Sparkle in the carrier. His paws and face were filthy. "What colour is your dog supposed to be?"

"He was white when I got him," said Sam as Amelia hid a grin. "I think he wants to play with Sparkle."

Tiffany sniffed again. "Well, Sparkle doesn't play with other dogs, *especially* not muddy ones."

She stalked off. But as she went, Sparkle looked down sadly at Mac, pawing at the carrier window and yapping noisily.

"Poor Sparkle," said Sam. "I bet he'd love to play in the puddles with Mac."

"Yes," said Amelia. "It's important for dogs to play with each other when they're young. I hope Tiffany knows what she's doing."

Sam shot Amelia a look that said he doubted it.

They hung posters in as many dry places as they could find. After they'd put one in the library, there was only one poster left – which they'd saved to put up at Animal Ark. They set off for the vet's. Inside, once they'd taken off their dripping jackets – and tried to get Mac to wipe his paws on the doormat – they hung up the poster, and were about to go through to the recovery room when Julia called out, "Good news!"

Amelia's heart lifted. "You've found the owner?"

The receptionist's face fell. "Not that, I'm afraid. We've found a sanctuary who can take the last kitten. They'll be coming to pick her up next week."

"Oh," said Amelia, trying to sound cheerful. "That's ... great news."

They left Mac with Julia, who dried his fur with a towel.

The dog found near the motorway was in a pen, her head resting on her paws. Her curly ears were drooping.

"Is she any better?" Amelia asked Mrs Hope, who was checking the poorly puppy's breathing with her stethoscope.

"We've confirmed that she needs an operation," said Mrs Hope. "She's still very ill."

"And no sign of the owner?" said Sam.

Mrs Hope shook her head. "I've just given the puppy a painkiller. That should make her more comfortable. Would you like to say hello? I'm sure she'd like to see some friendly faces."

Amelia stroked the puppy's head gently. She wagged her tail weakly. *If she does have an owner somewhere, she must be missing her terribly*, thought Amelia.

"Don't worry. We're going to help you," she said. "I promise."

CHAPTER FIVE

The next morning, Sam and Mac
arrived at Amelia's after breakfast. It
was still raining, and they were both
soaked through.

"Any news?" Sam asked, as they went
upstairs.

Amelia shook her head. Her mum

had let her phone Animal Ark first thing that morning to find out if the puppy's owner had come forward. But no one had got in touch.

Amelia felt as if she had a big weight in her tummy. The posters, the flyers … What if was all for nothing? She flopped on to the window seat in her bedroom. Sam slumped beside her and Mac lay at their feet.

"What are we going to do?" asked Sam with a groan. "If she was found by the motorway, the owner might not even live around here. They might never see our posters."

Amelia realised he was right. They sat for a long time, thinking about what to do. With every day that passed the dog's condition would get worse.

"We've got to save her," said Amelia. "So if we can't find the owner … we'll just have to pay for the operation ourselves!"

"But how?" asked Sam. "I haven't got two thousand pounds, and I'm guessing you haven't either."

Amelia twirled a lock of hair between her fingers, thinking hard. Suddenly, she remembered the conversation with the TV crew.

"You know what Mr Ferguson said yesterday? About motorbike shows?"

Sam nodded. "You should have seen him this morning," he said. "He wanted to show the film crew his motorbike. He kept going outside to see if they were around, but they weren't filming because of the rain. He *really* wants to be on telly. I saw him looking at himself out on the hall mirror, wearing his helmet and his leathers."

Amelia laughed. "What if we organised

a show of our own?" she said. "That way we might be able to get enough money!"

"A motorbike show?" Sam asked, looking confused.

"No, a dog show!" said Amelia. "We could charge for entry."

A grin spread across Sam's lips. "Brilliant idea!"

Two hours later, their friends Izzy and Josh were sitting in Amelia's bedroom. The floor was covered with pieces of paper they'd scribbled over, and there were mugs of hot chocolate by their sides. It was still pouring outside, with rain lashing the window, but the room was full of bright excitement.

"What have we got so far?" asked Josh.

Amelia read from her notebook, which was covered in animal stickers. "Date and time: Saturday at 10am. Location: Mr Stevens's barn."

"It was really nice of him to say we could have the show there," said Sam.

"My mum has got planks and poles to make the agility course," Izzy said. "And Mr Stevens has other stuff we can use for the events."

"My mum and Gran will collect the money at the door," said Amelia.

"Where's the list of events?" asked Josh.

Sam scooped up Mac and took the piece of paper he was sitting on. "Here it is! We've got Best Trick, Best Groomed Dog, Dog Most Like Its Owner, Best Paw Shaker, Waggiest Tail, Most Obedient and an Obstacle Course."

"This is going to be so much fun," said Amelia. "Now we just need contestants. We'll have to spread the word!"

"I can do that," said Josh.

"Me too!" said Izzy.

"And Sam and I can go to Animal Ark to ask the Hopes if they could be the judges," said Amelia. "Let's go!"

They all set off out into the rain. But that didn't bother Amelia one bit. She finally felt that they had a real chance to make a difference.

🐾 🐾 🐾 🐾

"What a good idea!" said Mrs Hope, after they'd explained their idea. "We'd love to be the judges – and we can even donate some prizes." She led them into the supply room. "We keep all the old stock in here. Tell us what you need, and we'll bring it to the show."

Sam clapped his hands. "Whoa! This room's like a doggy Aladdin's cave!"

Amelia gasped. There were dog chews, combs and brushes, packets of treats, collars, even dog baskets. She'd thought they could make rosettes for the winners, but this was even better! "Thank you!" she said.

"What you're doing is fantastic," said Mr Hope, but he wore an uncertain frown. "I just hope it's in time."

Amelia swallowed. *The dog show fundraiser has got to work – we have to save the puppy!*

"Back in a minute," she said to Sam. As the others made a list of the prizes,

Amelia slipped away to visit Star. She went through to the hotel. Before she even reached Star's pen, she heard the little kitten mewing. And when she came into view, Star was pawing at the mesh door.

"Hello!" said Amelia. She opened the pen and took out the kitten out. After a cuddle she set Star on the floor and found an old piece of string to play with. Star bounced around, flopping and skidding on the tiles. *She'd make such a lovely pet for someone*, thought Amelia.

She heard Sam calling that he'd finished with the list.

"Sorry, Star – I've got to go," she said. "But I'll come back and see you soon."

Putting the kitten back in the pen was so hard to do. Star watched her with big, shining eyes as she locked the door, and Amelia wanted to cry.

It was raining harder than ever as they made their way back to Amelia's house, and a gusting wind made her umbrella turn inside out. Sam was shivering. Only Mac didn't seem to mind – he was splashing in the puddles again, and snapping at the raindrops. When they rounded a corner, they saw the TV crew's van parked by the side of the road, with Freya Ward and the others beside it. Mr Ferguson was there too, with his motorbike.

"Maybe they're filming him," said Sam. "Let's go and find out."

But when they got closer, Amelia saw that they all looked worried. "Hi!" she said. "Is something wrong?"

Freya looked up from her plastic-covered clipboard, her soaking hair plastered to her head. "Hi, guys," she said. "I'm afraid so. Our equipment's waterproof, but we can't film in these conditions! And the rain's forecast to last all week. It's been a wasted trip."

"So we've had to cancel," said a man next to her. He was dismantling a camera from a tripod.

"Any luck finding the owner of that poorly puppy?" asked Freya.

"Not yet," said Amelia. "But we're organising a dog show to pay for her treatment."

"What a great idea," said the cameraman, packing his camera up.

Freya and the others finished loading their equipment away. "Good luck with it all!" she said, climbing into the front seat of the van.

Mac shook his wet fur, coating Mr Ferguson with droplets of water.

"Perhaps I could have a word with you?" Mr Ferguson said, shooting a glance at Amelia and Sam. "After the children have gone."

"Yes, of course," said the filmmaker.

As Amelia headed on to her house with Sam and Mac, she looked back and saw Mr Ferguson deep in conversation

59

with Freya through the window of the
TV crew's van.

"He really wants to get on TV!" she
said to Sam with a laugh.

CHAPTER SIX

On Saturday at half past nine, Amelia,
Sam and Mac arrived early at Spring
Farm to help get everything ready
for the dog show. It was *still* raining!
The last few days had passed in a blur
of organising. The local paper had
even agreed to put in a free advert to

promote the show, but Amelia had no idea how many people would come.

"I'm getting butterflies!" she said, as they walked up to the barn.

"Me too," said Sam.

The barn was bustling with activity. Izzy and her mum were putting the finishing touches to the obstacle course. At the far end of the barn, Mr Stevens and his sons were stacking bales of hay to make a winner's podium, and setting out other bales for people to sit on.

"This is amazing," said Amelia. "Thank you, everyone!"

Mr Stevens pointed to a bale of hay where Caramel the cat and her kitten, Snowdrop, were sitting together. "They've both settled in well," he said. Amelia remembered this was the same barn where they'd found Caramel. She looked so much healthier now that she was being looked after by Mr Stevens. Caramel and her kitten were both watching all the activity curiously.

"I'm not sure she's very happy to have her home invaded!" said Amelia.

"She'll make herself scarce when the dogs arrive, I would have thought," said Mr Stevens.

Josh was there too, with his parents. Then the Hopes arrived with the prizes. Amelia's mum and her gran stationed themselves at the barn door, ready to collect the entrance money from the spectators and competitors.

If anyone shows up, thought Amelia nervously.

But at ten to ten the first visitors started to appear. They came in a stream of people and dogs up the farm track. There were large dogs, small dogs, bouncy dogs and fluffy dogs. Amelia even spotted Tiffany carrying her backpack, with Sparkle's head sticking out of the back.

"Here they come!" said Sam. "It's time for the show to start!"

As her mum and gran collected the entrance fees, Amelia heard the rumble of an engine. Coming up the track was a motorbike, with Mr Ferguson astride it. However, there was another person on the back. Amelia frowned in confusion as they parked and the person on the back lifted off their helmet. It was Freya Ward! The filmmaker unloaded two large bags from the back of the bike, and headed towards them.

"Hello, you two," she said.

"I thought you'd left," said Amelia.

Freya smiled. "My crew have gone, but Mr Ferguson here persuaded me to stay on. I've agreed to film a segment about your dog show for the local television station."

Mr Ferguson went red. "I thought it might help spread the word about the missing puppy," he said. "Maybe the owner will see it on the evening news."

Amelia gaped at Sam. "That's amazing, Mr Ferguson!" she said.

Freya nodded to her bags. "I've got

some mobile equipment in here. Let me go inside and get set up!"

"Now, what are you doing for an announcer?" asked Mr Ferguson.

"We hadn't thought of that," said Sam.

Mr Ferguson puffed out his chest. "Well, look no further," he said. "I'm used to giving speeches at work. People say I'm rather good at it."

"Well, if you don't mind," said Amelia.

Mr Ferguson was already peeling off his leathers as he marched into the barn.

"He's going to be on TV after all!" Amelia laughed – "but so are we!"

Five minutes later they were ready to start. The dogs and their owners were sitting at the front, with all the other spectators crammed in behind. Freya had a tripod facing the show area, and Mr Ferguson was standing on top of a hay bale.

"Attention, ladies and gentlemen, dogs and puppies!" he boomed.

Amelia scanned the barn. She thought there were about two hundred people crowded inside – far more than she'd ever thought possible.

"It's time for our first event – the Best Trick," Mr Ferguson went on. "Contestants, please line up!"

The barn filled with yaps and
enthusiastic chatter, as dogs of all shapes
and sizes were led by their owners to
the middle. There was a huge Great
Dane and a tiny Chihuahua. There was
a black Labrador with a gentle face, a
Pug with a little
squashed nose, and
a Border Collie
with its tongue
hanging out. There
was a pair of
spaniels with long,

glossy ears. Behind them was a proud
Doberman, a silky-haired little Yorkshire
terrier, a sausage dog and an excited

Beagle. Some other dogs looked like
what Gran had once called "Bitsers" –
bits of everything. Amelia thought they
were all adorable.

"Contestants, get ready to
demonstrate your Best Trick," Mr
Ferguson called out. "Good luck, and
may the best dog win!"

First, a tall man and the Great Dane came forward. The man held up a cat basket. "Jasper's trick is that he can curl up in this!"

There was laughter from the spectators. Jasper was so big, his head came up to his owner's chest!

The tall man put the basket on the

ground. "Jasper," he ordered the dog. "Bed!"

Jasper put his front paws in the basket. Then he hunched his long body and put his back paws in too. He dipped his tail and sat. Very slowly, he folded his long front legs and somehow, miraculously, curled himself up. The cat basket vanished under his big body.

"Wow!" gasped Amelia.

Everyone clapped and cheered. The man gave Jasper a treat.

Next up was a woman and the tiny Chihuahua, who ran a miniature obstacle course by trotting *under* the jumps. She was followed by the Labrador, who was led by a little girl Amelia recognised from the reception class at school. The girl led the dog into the ring, shook hands with her solemnly and then led her out again. The girl's mum gave them both a treat. Then came the Pug, who "played dead" by lying very still with his paws in the air, and the Border Collie, who trotted around in time to the music his owner played on his phone.

After that came the two spaniels. Their owner, a man in a stripy hoodie, said, "Penzi, Laika, hug!" The two dogs faced each other, sitting up on their hind legs.

Then they rested their front paws on each other's shoulders, noses touching.

Amelia felt her heart melt. Applause and cries of "Aaahhhh!" sounded all around the barn.

A few more tricks followed, and last came the Dalmatian. Her owner, a woman with purple streaks in her hair, said, "Dotty! Hide!" Dotty barked and set off, running among the audience.

Sam scratched his head. "Um, was that the trick?"

"Oh no!" wailed Dotty's owner, hurrying after her. "She was meant to put her paw over her eyes!"

Everyone laughed. Mr and Mrs Hope went to speak to Mr Ferguson as the audience waited to hear their decision, buzzing with excitement. Mr Ferguson stood on the hay bale again.

"Ladies and gentlemen, puppies and dogs," he said, "thank you for showing us your Best Tricks! The winner of our first event is …"

A hush fell over the barn.

"… Mr Denny with Penzi and Laika!"

Amelia and Sam cheered loudly along with everyone else. Mr Denny led his spaniels over to the Hopes, who presented him with his prize – a squeaky toy for each of the dogs. Freya filmed the Hopes shaking Mr Denny's hand, and Penzi and Laika playing with their prizes.

"The fun has only just started," boomed Mr Ferguson. "Now it's time to find the Best Groomed Dog!"

The contestants began gathering in the centre of the barn. A woman in a yellow dress had a tall, elegant Afghan hound,

which had long, flowing fur. A round
man with a bald head brushed his St
Bernard's white, black and brown coat.
A teenage boy had a poodle with neat,
curly black fur. Tiffany stood with them,
looking very smug indeed. *She thinks
she's won already*, thought Amelia. Tiffany
placed her rucksack carefully on a hay
bale. Sparkle's ears were pricked up.

"Time for your moment to shine!"
Tiffany told her dog.

As she unfastened the zip on the
backpack, Sparkle climbed out and
shook himself. He stared at the barn
door, yapped excitedly, and sprang off
the hay bale.

"Sparkle – no!" said Tiffany. But it was too late. Sparkle had set off running for the door. "Come back!" Tiffany squealed.

"I wonder what Sparkle has seen," muttered Amelia.

Sam glanced around. "Uh-oh … where's Mac?"

They both set off, sprinting after Sparkle and Tiffany.

When they reached the door, Tiffany was standing with her hand over her mouth, almost in tears. There, in a big muddy puddle, were the two dogs. It was hard to tell them apart, because their fur was matted to their bodies with brown mud. The only other colour was the occasional flash of an eye or pink tongue as they rolled around, happily playing. Sparkle's blue ribbon was floating on the surface.

"*Sparkle!*" Tiffany whimpered. "Look at the state of you!"

Her little dog scampered out of the mud, and trotted over, dripping wet. He didn't seem to care at all.

"Maybe you can clean him up a bit?" said Sam.

Tiffany glared at him, then pointed at Mac. "It's your puppy's fault! Sparkle would never have dreamed of rolling around in the mud if your mucky pup hadn't made him do it!"

She put a lead on Sparkle's filthy collar and stalked off. Sparkle looked back at them over his shoulder, straining to get back to the puddle with Mac.

"Poor Tiffany," giggled Amelia. "But at least Sparkle had fun!"

CHAPTER SEVEN

They went back inside, where the
Afghan hound was being declared the
winner of the 'Best Groomed' event.
Tiffany, doing her best to clean Sparkle,
pouted crossly as the Afghan's owner
collected the prize – a pretty gold-
coloured collar.

"Congratulations, Ms Taylor and Portia," said Mr Ferguson. "Next up is the Dog Who Looks Most Like Its Owner contest!"

"This should be funny," said Sam. "The show's going really well, isn't it?"

Amelia nodded. "I keep thinking about the poorly puppy, though," she said. "I just hope we raise enough money to make her well again."

Lots of dogs and owners entered the

lookalike event. The winner was a white, curly-haired poodle and her owner, a lady with curly blonde hair.

82

Next came the Agility event. It included a bridge made from planks, an arch of flowerpots, traffic cones to weave around, a maze of hay bales, and at the end a hula hoop for the dogs to jump through. A well-trained sheepdog owned by a neighbouring farmer got to the finish line first and claimed the prize.

"We've got much more fun to come." Mr Ferguson boomed. "Don't miss the Musical Stays, Best Paw Shaker and Waggiest Tail events! But up next, it's Obedience!"

Sam bit his lip nervously. "I've entered Mac in this one," he said.

"He'll be brilliant," Amelia reassured him. She gave Mac a good luck hug – his muddy fur was drying into spikes. She spotted Sam's parents in the audience, sitting on one of the hay bales. "Look, your mum and dad are here to watch you."

"That's what I'm worried about," said Sam gloomily. "What if Mac messes up? They'll think he's still too naughty and I'll have to give him up."

"Don't think about that," Amelia told him. "Just do your best."

But her heart was racing as she watched Sam and Mac make their way to the showing area. Several other dogs and their owners lined up beside them.

"Ready, set … May the best dog win!" called Mr Ferguson.

Mr Hope stood next to the line of dogs. "First, please ask your dogs to walk to the traffic cone, then to sit," he instructed them.

The owners began coaxing their dogs.

"Walkies, Violet!" a woman told her slender whippet.

"Come on, Pearl!" a man called to a little white dog.

"Heel, Mac! Good boy!" said Sam, hurrying along in front of his puppy. When they reached the cone, he said, "Sit!" Mac immediately sat down, tucking his front paws neatly together.

"Well done, Mac!" Amelia called.

So far, so good ...

The other dogs sat down too.

"Ask your dogs to walk to this traffic cone, then roll over," said Mr Hope.

"Heel, Mac!" said Sam, and the other owners called their dogs too. They all walked neatly to the cone and rolled over, showing their tummies.

"Very good," said Mr Hope. "Now for the final part of the challenge. The dogs must follow you through the maze of traffic cones, then jump through the hula hoop. The first dog to jump through the hoop is the winner!"

Amelia held her breath as they set off. Sam's face was furrowed with concentration as he guided Mac through the maze of cones. When Amelia glanced over towards his parents, Mr Baxter looked anxious,

while Mrs Baxter had her hands clasped in front of her. Mac followed Sam, zigzagging through the cones, his tail wagging. They were in the lead when they reached the hula hoop, which was suspended from the roof beams by a rope. Amelia could hardly watch.

"Jump, Mac!" Sam commanded.

Mac crouched down, his ears back …

The crowd went silent, everyone's attention focused on Sam's dog.

You can do it! Amelia willed from the sidelines.

But Mac stayed put. One by one, the other dogs reached the hoops and jumped through, leaving Sam and Mac on the other side.

Sam looked close to tears as he sadly picked Mac up. Amelia was barely listening as Mr Ferguson announced the winner was Mrs Evans and her Wire-haired Terrier, Scamp. She rushed to her friend's side. Mac was licking his face, oblivious.

"You did really well!" she said.

"He didn't know what to do," said Sam sadly. "He's never even seen a hoop before."

Sam's smiling parents arrived. "That was amazing, Sam!" said Mr Baxter.

"And we're so impressed with Mac," said Sam's mum. "In fact, he's a changed puppy since you starting training him. No more chewing, no more accidents."

"And Mr Ferguson hasn't complained about him in days!" added Mr Baxter.

A slow smile spread across Sam's face. "Does that mean … we can keep him?" asked Sam. His dark brown eyes were wide and pleading.

Amelia held her breath. *Please say yes*, she thought, *please …*

"Of course!" said Mrs Baxter. "Sam, we would never be able to give Mac up, even if he was the naughtiest dog in Yorkshire. He's part of the family now!"

"YES!" shouted Sam. "Thank you, thank you, thank you!" Mac barked and nuzzled him so enthusiastically that Sam toppled over, and they both sprawled on the barn floor. Bits of straw stuck in Sam's hair and Mac's fur.

They made a fuss of Mac and fed him treats while the show continued. A Labrador won Waggiest Tail, a Wire-Haired Pointer took the prize for Musical Stays, freezing on the spot, and Best Paw Shaker went to a Husky. Amelia was surrounded by all kinds of dogs and enjoying every second.

Following the final event, Mr Ferguson called for silence. "Ladies and gentlemen," he boomed, "pups and pooches! Thank you all for coming today. As you know, it was for a good cause. All the money raised today is going towards the treatment of a very poorly puppy currently being looked after by the hard-working vets at Animal Ark."

Mum and Gran arrived at his side. Mum was holding a box they'd collected the money in, and she beckoned Amelia and Sam over. She hugged them both. "You two should announce the amount," she whispered, "as you're the reason we're here."

Gran winked at them, and handed Amelia a slip of paper with the grand total written on it. Amelia and Sam both gasped.

"Amelia and Sam," said Mr Ferguson, "Can you please tell everyone how much we've made today?"

Together, they read, "One thousand, eight hundred and sixteen pounds!"

Cheers went up around the barn, but as they died down, Amelia realised the horrible truth.

"It's still not enough," she muttered.

Mrs Hope raised her voice, so

everyone could hear. "We should all be inspired by Amelia and Sam," she said. "They've shown that when the village comes together, anything is possible. Animal Ark will donate the rest of the money so that we can give our patient the best possible care. Thank you to everyone here – and a huge, special thank you to the two amazing animal lovers who organised all of this: Amelia and Sam!"

The barn erupted with applause and barks. Amelia and Sam grinned at each other. Amelia could feel herself blushing with happiness, and it was the best feeling in the world.

CHAPTER EIGHT

"Congratulations, guys!" said Freya Ward. "What an amazing show. We've got loads of great footage for the local news – but I'd really love to interview you too. What do you think?"

Amelia and Sam grinned at each other. "We'll do it!" said Amelia.

A few minutes later, they were sitting on a hay bale while Freya positioned her camera.

A cloud of nervous butterflies started to flutter in Amelia's stomach. Sam was jiggling around beside her, and she could tell he was anxious too. The only person who seemed at ease was Mac. He was sitting patiently at Sam's feet.

"There we are," said Freya. She came to sit beside them in front of the camera, clutching a microphone. "Are you two ready?"

They both nodded. Freya started by giving a brief introduction to the dog show, then turned to face them.

"I'm with Amelia Heywood and Sam Baxter, the organisers of the show," Freya said.

"And Mac," added Sam. Mac barked and wagged his tail.

"And Mac," said Freya with a laugh. "So, tell us – what inspired you to put together this amazing show?"

"It all started when a lady brought a

puppy into Animal Ark," Amelia began. "That's the vet's here in Welford …"

She explained how the puppy needed an operation, with Sam chipping in every so often. As she spoke, Amelia felt her nerves melt away – this was her chance to help the puppy again.

"We've raised enough money for the puppy to have her operation," Amelia said, "but we still need to find her owner. Could we show all the viewers a photo of her? Then if anyone knows who she is they can phone Animal Ark."

"That's a wonderful plan," said Freya. "We'll be sure to put all those details up on screen. Amelia, Sam –

congratulations on organising such a wonderful dog show!"

The filming was over. "I really hope it works," Amelia said to Sam.

The puppy had her operation two days later. It took several hours, and Amelia could hardly think about anything else. Mr Hope had told them that any procedure was risky, and the fact it was a puppy only made it more so.

At school, she found herself staring out of the window, wondering how the patient was getting on. She could tell from the way Sam chewed his nails in class that he was thinking about it too. Then, at the school gates, Sam's mum met them and said they were going straight to Animal Ark.

"Is the puppy all right?" she asked.

"I don't know," said Mrs Baxter.

At the vet's, Julia led them through to the recovery room. Lying on a blanket in a pen was the puppy. There were raised red stitches on her shaved tummy, and she was wearing a cone-shaped collar to stop her from licking them. But her eyes were bright, and she wagged her tail when Amelia leaned in and patted her head.

"She's a changed puppy," said Mr

Hope, arriving with his wife. "She's recovering better than we expected."

Mrs Hope nodded. "She's a tough little thing. She still needs lots of care, but she'll be running around in no time!"

Amelia and Sam both grinned at this.

"That's brilliant!" said Amelia.

"So cool!" said Sam.

Mr and Mrs Hope glanced at each other. "You might be wondering why we brought you here," said Mrs Hope. Her eyes were shining. She opened the door to the waiting room. "Miss Cook?" she called. "Would you like to come through to meet Amelia and Sam?"

A young woman came into the room, using crutches to help her walk. Her ankle was encased in a large, sturdy boot.

"Miss Cook is the puppy's owner," explained Mr Hope with a smile.

Amelia stared at Miss Cook in amazement.

"Oh, wow!" cried Sam.

"It's so lovely to meet you," said the lady. "I saw you talking about Ninja on the news, but I couldn't collect her until today because of my broken leg. She escaped from her dog-sitter when I was in hospital – she must have tried to find her way home!" Her eyes were glistening with tears. "Thank you so much for saving her. I really can't thank you both enough!"

Amelia was so happy, she felt as if

she was soaring like a bird. "We loved helping her," she said.

Mr and Mrs Hope helped place Ninja carefully in a travelling basket, and took her out to where Miss Cook's friend was waiting with a car. Amelia and Sam stood in the Animal Ark doorway and waved them off. "Bye!" Sam called.

"Bye, Ninja!" added Amelia. "Get well soon!"

When they'd driven away, Julia turned to Amelia and Sam. "The best news is that Miss Cook has pet insurance that will cover the cost of the operation!"

The news startled Amelia. "So we

raised all that money for nothing?"

"Not at all," said Julia. "There are lots of dog charities that would be more than happy to receive a donation. You could help dozens of dogs instead of just one!"

Sam grinned at Amelia. "And I reckon we could do a show like that every year if we wanted."

"I'd love to!" she replied.

Mrs Hope called across the reception. "Would you mind both coming back here for a moment?" she asked. "We'd like to talk to you about something." Her expression was serious.

What could it be? Amelia wondered.

CHAPTER NINE

The Hopes led them through to the consulting room.

"We're so impressed with you both," said Mrs Hope. "In the past few weeks, you've rescued kittens, helped a rabbit and saved a fox. And now you've made sure Ninja got the treatment she needed."

"Amelia," Mr Hope went on, "when you first came to Welford, you said you'd like to help out at Animal Ark. At the time, we weren't sure you could cope with the hard work and responsibility. Well, we've been talking about it – and we've decided we were wrong."

Amelia swallowed. She felt Sam tense at her side.

"You've both more than proved yourselves," Mrs Hope went on. "So how would you like to help out properly at Animal Ark?"

Amelia and Sam grabbed each other, jumping up and down, whirling around and grinning. Mr and Mrs Hope laughed.

"Is that a yes?" asked Mr Hope.

"Yes, yes, yes!" said Amelia, when she'd caught her breath. "Thank you!"

"This is the best thing ever!" added Sam happily.

"Then that settles it," said Mrs Hope. "You're official Animal Ark volunteers!

We'll talk to your parents and then we can draw up a proper rota so we know when you're coming in."

As the vets both went off to handle their next appointments, Sam and Amelia remained in the reception. Amelia's cheeks were sore from smiling so much. "I'd better go home and take Mac for a walk," said Sam. "See you here tomorrow!"

He said goodbye to Julia and set off. Amelia was about to go too, when she remembered Star. Back in the hotel section, Simon the nurse was cleaning one of the pens. Amelia said hello and went over to Star's pen.

It was empty.

"She's gone," said Simon.

"To the sanctuary?" asked Amelia.

Simon shook his head. "I think they found an adopter, actually. I'm not sure who."

Amelia wanted to ask, but Mr and Mrs Hope were both with patients, and Julia was busy at reception. Not that it really mattered, as long as Star had a good home.

Amelia knew she shouldn't feel sad, but she couldn't help it. *I didn't even get to say goodbye.*

She walked out of Animal Ark and back home. It had finally stopped raining and golden sunlight started to reach through the clouds. As she let herself in the front door, her mum called from the kitchen.

"Hello, darling! How was school and Animal Ark?"

Amelia could tell her about the puppy later. Right now, she just wanted to be on her own.

"It was OK," she replied.

She went up to her room, and through the window she saw the gleam of a rainbow curving over the village.

It seemed such a long time since she'd moved to Welford, though it had only been a few weeks. She'd been so worried she wouldn't make friends. But now she had Sam and Mac, and Josh and Izzy. And she'd proved herself to the Hopes – she could look forward to many happy days helping out at Animal Ark, caring for the patients.

Her mind wandered back to Star. She really hoped she had found a perfect home …

"Amelia?" It was Mum, peeking in through a crack in the door. "There's someone here to see you."

Wondering who it could be, she went out to the landing and saw her mum waiting there. She was smiling.

"Is it Sam?" Amelia asked.

"Downstairs, in the living room," said Mum. More confused than ever, Amelia descended to the ground floor. Through the living room door, she could see Gran on the sofa, but no one else.

"What's going on?" she said.

Then she saw it. The little tortoiseshell kitten curled in a basket on the rug.

"Star!" Amelia cried.

"Star?" Mum asked.

"That's what I've been calling her," Amelia said, shyly. "But what's she doing here?" Then the smiles on Mum and Gran's faces made her realise. Her heart soared. "We've adopted her? Really?"

"Yes, really," said Mum, her eyes shining brightly.

Amelia crouched down, taking Star gently in her hands and holding the kitten's soft furry cheek to her own. Star began to purr.

"What about when I'm at Dad's?" Amelia asked. She spent every other weekend with her dad in York.

"Gran and I will look after her," Mum said. "It's no problem."

"You've spent so much time helping other people's pets that we thought you should have one of your own," said Gran. "Everyone could see you two have a special connection."

Amelia could hardly believe it. She hugged Mum and Gran and Star, all at the same time. "Thank you so much!" she cried.

Amelia took Star to the sofa and sat down with the kitten on her lap. What an amazing day it had been! Ninja finding her owner, Mr and Mrs Hope saying that Amelia could be an official helper, and now this. She couldn't wait to tell Sam.

Star climbed up her front, nuzzled under Amelia's chin, then rolled back on to the cushions. Amelia tickled her tummy as the kitten boxed the air with her paws.

"She likes that!" said her mum.

Amelia couldn't believe Star was

actually hers. Everything was just *perfect*!

The End

Turn the page for a sneak peek at
Amelia and Sam's next adventure!

ANiMAL ARK

Two
adventures in
One!

The Purrfect Sleepover

Lucy Daniels

Amelia and Sam began their search on the patio. Mac followed them around, sniffing at the bikes and flower pots. When Sam peered under a bushy plant, Mac lay down and looked there too. When Sam shifted a loose coil of hosepipe, Mac pounced on it and gave it a shake.

Amelia's chest got tighter with worry every minute. At last, she flopped down on a white plastic chair. "This is awful, Sam. We're supposed to be looking after Luna, not losing her!"

Sam fist-bumped her shoulder. "Hey! Don't give up. I know – maybe Mac can sniff her out!" He picked up one of

Luna's garden toys and held it out to Mac. "Here, Mac. This is Luna's smell. Where is she, boy?"

Mac gave the toy a sniff, and a lick for good measure, then padded around the garden.

"Yip!" Mac jumped up at the cherry tree, resting his front paws on the smooth brown trunk. "Yip!"

"He's found her!" cried Sam.

Amelia peered up into the branches and gave a sigh of relief. "Luna!" she whispered. "There you are!" The grey kitten was crouched, shivering, on a branch. But something was wrong. Her fur was matted into damp tufts, and her eyes were huge. The black pupils in the middle were so wide and round that only a thin circle of blue showed around them.

The cat let out a sad meow.

Amelia kept her voice soft and low. "Don't worry, Luna. We'll get you down."

Sam brought over the plastic garden chair, and Amelia stood on it and reached up for the kitten. "Come on, Luna," she coaxed. "Don't be frightened."

Luna seemed to remember that Amelia was a friend. With another anxious *meow*, the kitten edged along the branch and let Amelia pick her up. Amelia passed her to Sam and climbed down from the chair.

She could see straight away that there was a deep scratch and a missing patch of fur on Luna's head. And when she ran her hands over the kitten's body she felt Luna flinch. Amelia's stomach knotted anxiously. "She's got scratches all over. I think she was in the cat fight I heard last night. She must have hid in the tree to escape the other cat." Amelia looked up at Sam. "We need to get her to Animal Ark straight away!"

Read **The Purrfect Sleepover**
to find out what happens next...

Animal Advice

Do you love animals as much as Amelia and Sam? Here are some tips on how to look after them from veterinary surgeon Sarah McGurk.

Caring for your pet

1. Animals need clean water at all times.
2. They need to be fed too – ask your vet what kind of food is best, and how much the animal needs.
3. Some animals, such as dogs, need exercise every da
4. Animals also need lots of love. You should always be very gentle with your pets and be careful not to anything that might hurt them.

When to go to the vet

metimes animals get ill. Like you, they will mostly get

tter on their own. But if your pet has hurt itself or

ms very unwell, then a trip to the vet might be needed.

me pets also need to be vaccinated, to prevent them

m getting dangerous diseases. Your vet can tell you

Helping wildlife

Always ask an adult before you go near any animals

you don't know.

If you find an animal or bird which is injured or can't

move, it is best not to touch it.

If you are worried, you can phone an animal charity

such as the RSPCA (SSPCA in Scotland) for help.